LEGEND

A Short By
JIMMY DASAINT

LEGEND

Published by:
DASAINT ENTERTAINMENT
Po Box 97 Bala Cynwyd, PA 19004

Website: www.dasaintentertainment.com

"Watch and pray, lest you enter into temptation. The spirit indeed is willing, but the flesh is weak."

-Matthew 26:41

"To live is to suffer.
To survive is to find the meaning in the suffering."

CHAPTER 1
WEST PHILLY

The pungent smell of crack cocaine hovered through the hallways of a dilapidated building. A small group of men and women sat in a circle passing around a tiny glass pipe.

"Yo Legend! Yo Legend!" a male's voice called out.

The man rushed down the hallway and entered a back room. Seeing his cousin, Legend, shock, and sadness consumed him as he shook his head in disappointment.

"What's up, Jimmy?" Legend said, passing the glass pipe to a woman who sat beside him.

"You forgot we have a game today? We play the Raiders!"
"Oh shit! I forgot all about the game, Jimmy," Legend replied.
"Well come on, man and don't worry about a jersey and shorts. I got an extra set."
"Okay, just let me get one more hit," Legend said, grabbing the pipe back from the woman beside him.

Legend placed a small piece of crack rock inside the cylinder, and then he lit it up with his lighter. After placing the pipe to his crusted lips, he inhaled the powerful drug into his veteran lungs. The small crowd watched, wishing they each could take the next hit, as Legend's blurry eyes drifted off to the back of his head. On the exhale, the strong fumes escaped into the air and Jimmy passed the pipe to another addict, before walking out of the abandoned building with Jimmy.

The duo got inside of a double-parked black Ford Taurus, and Jimmy quickly sped down the street.

"Thanks, man, for coming to get me."

"No problem cuz. But seriously, when are you gonna leave them drugs alone?" Jimmy asked, sincerely.

Legend pondered the thought momentarily, before looking over at his younger cousin and said, "When they leave me alone because so far my demons won't let 'em. They got a crazy hold on me cuz."

Leon "Legend" Shaw was a tall, slender, dark-skinned man. Standing at 6'5 with a head full of wavy hair and hazel brown eyes, Legend was known for his good looks. He was quite the ladies' man before his crack addiction took hold of him. After becoming a crack addict, not only had his looks suffered, but his basketball skills diminished as well.

Legend was considered the best ballplayer in Philly. He had no competition, and his reputation was far-reaching.

Upon graduating from West Philly High, Legend was considered one of the top, uncommitted freshmen ballers in the nation. Every college in the nation wanted him to play for their team. It was a tough choice to make with countless colleges trying to recruit the young, rising star, but in the end, Legend chose Duke University; located in Durham, North Carolina.

During his freshman year, Legend averaged 19.7 points and 8.4 rebounds a game. He even won Rookie of the Year honors in the Men's Atlantic Coast Conference (A.C.C.) Basketball Tournament.

Soon after his basketball successes, things began to fall apart for the promising NBA lottery pick. Legend got involved with drugs to handle the pressures of success and was expelled from school. He lost his four-year scholarship after countless warnings from his couch and two drug violations. The college superstar was given a one-way ticket back to Philly, and his life as a future basketball icon, filled with money, women, and fame changed overnight. And, since then, Legend has become a crack addict who had lost all hope, promise, and direction. He is a former shell of himself who views life as everything except fair.

"Yo, just change your clothes in the back seat. We gotta hurry up," Jimmy said, as Legend climbed into the backseat and changed into his uniform.

Jimmy, who was twenty-four and Legend's younger cousin, loved the ground Legend walked on. No matter the situation Legend got into, or the time of day he was in need, Jimmy would do anything in his power to help out his big cousin. They were like brothers.

Jimmy was a genuine, upstanding young man. He was 5'10, light brown skinned, with a solid, muscular, yet athletic body, and he was one helluva point guard. Legend had been Jimmy's greatest teacher, and during the summer and winter leagues, Legend kept Jimmy's skill sharp coaching and encouraging his younger cousin to play his best. When

Legend wasn't too high, and Jimmy could find him, they played alongside each other.

"We should be there in ten minutes," Jimmy said. "It don't matter, just get me there. I'm ready to ball," Legend smiled.

CHAPTER 2
FIFTEEN MINUTES LATER
48TH STREET PLAYGROUND
WEST PHILLY

A large blusterous crowd of fans and onlookers gathered around the small basketball court. A local DJ had his large, high powered speakers stacked on top of one another as the lyrics and beats of one of Meek Mills popular songs blasted out the woofers. The two basketball teams were getting ready to play in the fourth quarter. The score was 58 to 50, and the Raiders were leading. Their star center, Calvin "Swish" Cheney had already scored thirty points.

"Five minutes fellas," the ref yelled out at both teams.

Suddenly the black Ford Taurus pulled up, and a young teenaged boy shouted, "Legend is here! The Legend just pulled up!"

The crowd went crazy- as they watched Legend and Jimmy rush out the car onto the court.

"Yo, Coach, you got our names in the books?" Jimmy asked, already assured of the answer.

"Yup, now I need y'all to go do what y'all do," Coach Jones said with a big smile plastered on his face.

Coach was happy that two of his best players had made it in time to play the game, even if it was the last quarter.

"They can't do that! They ain't play the whole game," the opposing coach frustratingly shouted.

"Yes, they can! Now get back over to your bench before I tech you Larry. You know their names were in the books," the ref said.

Even if the opposing coach had a legit gripe with Legend and Jimmy entering the game in the last quarter, the ref wasn't trying to hear it. The ref and the crowd were big-time fans of Leon "Legend" Shaw. Whenever he was on the court, he got mad respect. He was a basketball icon in the hood, with a game so smooth that people referred to Legend as the second coming of Michael Jordan.

CHAPTER 3

"Don't get scared now! Y'all had y'all fun," Legend yelled to the opposing bench.

"Fuck you! You crackhead!" Swish shouted back.

Legend smiled and walked onto the court. Name calling didn't bother him even though the unpopular title was accurate. Everyone knew Legend's background and the story about his fall from grace. He had been a basketball prodigy since the age of twelve and was featured in *SLAM* and *Sports Illustrated Magazine* as the second coming of Michael Jordan. Legend was that good and when he didn't make it to the status of those greats, his city hurt because they were all rooting for him.

After the referee passed the ball to Jimmy, he quickly inbounded the ball to Legend. Legend was ready as his defender, who was a few inches shorter, came up on him. Standing at the top of the key, Legend released a long three-pointer.

SWISH and just like that, it was *ALL NET*! The crowd went off!

After another defensive stop, Jimmy brought the ball up the court and quickly passed it to his cousin. This time Swish was guarding Legend. They stood around the same height, so on paper, it was an even match up. But Swish knew, despite the fact that Legend smoked crack, he was a baller, always.

Swish was overmatched and his physical talents weren't enough to stop Legend. Legend quickly dribbled the ball through Swish's legs, and as soon as Swish reached for the ball Legend crossed him over and went straight up to the basket. A shorter defender tried to take a charge, but Legend euro-stepped around him and Tomahawk dunked the ball. Once again, the crowd went wild as the tide of the game quickly changed. The once confident Raiders were now showing signs of fear as their assumed win was fleeting.

After the Raiders called for a quick time out, Legend walked over to Coach Jones.

> "Coach, do they got my money?"
> "Yup, and if we can beat them bums by five, then Chucks said he'd give you a bonus."
> "Enough said," Legend replied as he walked away smiling.

Something caught Legend's attention as he looked over by the fence and saw two men with their gaze upon him. Chuck and Mack were two of the big-time drug dealers from the neighborhood. Every game Legend played in; they placed substantial bets on the game.

> "Beat'em by five, and we got something nice for you," Chuck shouted to Legend.

Legend winked at the men and said, "Have that ready for me."

As he looked around the court, he noticed a kid staring at him with a stoic face. For a moment, Legend froze, before rushing to join his team.

"Let's get these bums out of here," Jimmy said.

For the next twelve minutes, Legend put on a one-man show. He hit three-pointer after three-pointer and even found time to throw down a devastating dunk. Watching Legend play was seeing a man amongst boys. He was that work, and when the smoke had cleared, Legend had twenty-six points, five rebounds, and three assists, leading his team to another win.

Once again, Legend's skills had spoken, and everyone in the crowd had witnessed another win that would add to his legacy.

However, despite everyone else's enthusiasm about Legend's basketball performance, he had other interest.

Legend raced over to Chuck and Mack. Sweaty and with his breathing labored, he said, "You got that?"

Chuck reached into his pocket and pulled out a fresh hundred dollar bill.

"Thanks," Legend said as he hurried and grabbed the money.

"Where's my bonus?" he said in all seriousness.

Mack reached into his pocket and then slowly withdrew his right hand. Inside his closed fist was a small rock of cocaine. It was an eight ball wrapped tightly in a small clear Ziploc bag. He passed the narcotic to Legend, and no sooner than it reached his hand, he quickly turned and walked away.

"Damn, what a waste," Chuck said. "He could've been the next Magic Johnson if he didn't fuck his life up," he continued.

The two men got into Chuck's fiery red BMW and sped off down the street.

Legend had tunnel vision as he walked to an abandoned building nearby. Once inside, he removed a small glass pipe and a slightly used pack of matches from his socks. Then, suddenly, a small shadow appeared, and Legend was startled as he jumped back.

"It's me, dad, Lil Leon," the young child's voice said softly. Legend quickly concealed his self-prescribed medicine behind his back.

"Hey, Lil man! What's going on?"

"Jimmy told me you had a game today, so I wanted to come see you play. I followed you here because I wanted to tell you that you're my favorite player in the whole world."

Legend gave his young son a quick hug and said, "And you're my favorite person in the world. Do you need anything? Is your mom okay?" Rushing to end his current conversation because the drugs were calling to him.

"We're good."

Legend reached his hand out and said, "Here, this is a hundred dollars. Give it to your mom and tell her I said I love her."

"I will, Dad. Guess what?"

"What?"
"My birthday is…"
"Friday, July 16th, and you'll be thirteen. I'll never forget that," Legend said, surprising the young boy because he remembered.
"I'm going to see you in a few days. We've got to practice that jump shot again, but get home because it's getting late."

After a quick hug, Leon sadly walked away. Leon knew his father was on drugs, and it hurt the young boy. He saw how the drugs had changed his father, and there was a great distance between them. Even though they lived in the same neighborhood, having a father on drugs- is not the same as having a father who lives in the home with his child and who is present in the raising of his young seed.

Legend, knew his son was disappointed but he was ready to get his reward. As the darkness crept to the forefront of the city, Legend strongly inhaled the crack into his lungs. It was everything he wanted, but everything he did not need. A tear of sorrow suffocated in guilt ran down Legend's face as his truth tried to invade his space.

At thirty-two, legend had a life filled with tragedy. When Legend was nine years old, an age where children are in great need of parental love and guidance, his parents were killed in a catastrophic car accident on Roosevelt Boulevard. He numbed his pain by focusing all of his time and attention on the courts. He ate, slept, and breathed basketball. It kept him calm, and his family encouraged him to stay at it because they noticed it helped him grieve. What they did not see was the pain he hid. Basketball didn't help him mourn; it only hid it.

The more Legend thought about his life, his mistakes, and his inability to kick his drug habit, the more he no longer wanted to think. He took another pull on his crack pipe to numb his reality. It was the cure he needed, and although it didn't last long, for the moment, he was healed of all his pains and worries.

CHAPTER 4
A FEW HOURS LATER

"How was the game?" Aunt Rose asked Jimmy.

"It was good, actually. We won."

"Did Leon play? Or did you have trouble finding him? " she said, fixing a plate of food.

"Yeah, he played."

"Where did you find him at this time? In somebody's car, a McDonald's' bathroom or in another abandoned building?" Aunt Rose asked, clearly disappointed with Legend's life choices.

"Mom, please stop. That's family," Jimmy sighed.

Aunt Rose placed their plates on the table and sat down beside her son. Jimmy was her only child, and Aunt Rose knew talking about Leon was tough for him.

"Baby are you still upset with me for putting him out the house?"

"Mom, you could've given him another chance, he's sick!"

"I gave Leon too many chances! And each time he took advantage of me and our home! He stole everything that wasn't nailed down! My TV's, jewelry, shoes, bags, and my money! I love Leon like a son, but enough is enough. That boy ruined his life! Not me, he did it to himself, and I refuse to let him back in this home again! I'm sorry Jimmy, but until Leon gets some help and gets off of them drugs, he can't come back here."

Jimmy put his face inside of his hands. He knew his mom was right, but the truth still hurt. Legend couldn't be trusted in their home, and if they let him back in, he would steal, again. Legend had proved that point when he recently asked to use the bathroom and walked out with Jimmy's new Jordan's and his Nike sweat suit. Still, Jimmy loved his big cousin no matter what he had done. Legend was family, and he held onto the hope that one day, he would rise above his addiction. Jimmy believed his cousin could one day live in a home and be done with the life of abandoned buildings filled with junkies. Jimmy held onto that belief, and it hurt deeply every time Legend proved to be closer to defeat than success.

After dinner, Jimmy made a plate of food and placed it into a plastic food container. Before he walked out the door, his mother said, "Tell Leon I love him," before walking up the stairs.

Aunt Rose was appointed Legend's legal guardian ever since his parents had died in the car accident. Seeing her nephew at the very bottom of the pit- killed her on the inside. Aunt Rose put up a tough act, but the pain of knowing she was losing Leon to his addiction ate at her core.

Inside her bedroom, Aunt Rose kneeled and began to pray.

"Lord, thank you for all the blessings you have bestowed upon me. Without your guidance and love, I am nothing. I pray to you, Lord, that you would bless and watch over my son and my nephew. Lord, they need your protection out there on those streets. I ask that you to continue to guide me in the right direction and down the right path and that you show Leon a different way, Lord!

Give him the strength to walk away from his addiction. Remove the Devil's grip from my Leon. He is a good man, Lord, who has lost his way. He needs your guidance and mercy, Lord. Please, please, please, Lord, if you can hear my cry, please show him the way before these streets take him from me forever. In Jesus name, I pray, father God, Amen!"

CHAPTER 5
LATER THAT NIGHT

Darkness fell over the city like a thick blanket, and the loud police sirens could be heard a mile away. It was late, and the only people out on the streets were addicts, searching for their fix. Philadelphia was in crisis as the drug epidemic tore through the city, breaking up families and destroying the lives of many citizens without warning. The hospitals were overflowing with patients who had overdosed, and some were not lucky enough to pull through. The war on drugs-was just a title because the country was losing the war, and had been losing countless lives for years.

Jimmy pulled up and parked his Ford Taurus in front of an abandoned building on 42nd and Girard Avenue. When he exited his car, he was holding a plastic plate of food wrapped in foil which he had made for Legend. This was a part of Jimmy's nightly routine, and it provided him with a sense of satisfaction to ensure Legend ate.

Jimmy walked up to the front door, which was hanging on the hinges, and yelled out, "Yo Legend. Yo cuz you in there?" When he didn't hear anything, he walked inside.

The house was disgusting. It was filled with garbage, dirty clothes, flying insects, roaches, mice, crack vials, used needles, and countless empty match booklets. Jimmy tightly held his nose to avoid the horrible smell that lingered throughout the house as he navigated his way through, to find his cousin.

"Yo Legend, where you at?"
"I'm back here."

Jimmy walked through the reeking hallway and went straight to a back room. When he entered the room, he saw Legend laying across an old dirty mattress, cuddled up with a female acquaintance. It was easy to see that before her addiction, this woman was gorgeous. Her facial beauty was still present, but her body had succumbed to the thinning and wear and tear of crack addiction.

"Thanks, cuz, this is my girl, Nicki."
"Hi Nicki," Jimmy said, as he passed Legend his plate of food.
"My mom said she loves you. You gotta come by the house one day- she misses you. Plus, it's been a few months since she last saw you."
"I'll think about it," Legend said, brushing Jimmy's request off.
"Here you go, babe, you can share some of this good food with me," Legend said, passing the plate of fried chicken, rice, collard greens, and yams over to Nicki.
"Thanks, Daddy," Nicki said not hesitating to dig in.

"You did good today Legend! They couldn't stop you at all. I think you broke the playground record for the most points in a quarter. And Coach was a little upset that you showed up late, but he was happy we got another win."

"It's cool, and as long as they got my money I'll be there," Legend said, taking a big bite out of a piece of the fried chicken.

Jimmy reached into his pocket and pulled out a small brochure.

"Here, you should check this out. It's not far from us."

Legend grabbed the booklet and took a glance at it before tossing it away.

"Not another drug rehab! Come on cuz! Why do you keep trying to change me?" "I'm trying to save you, Legend! Look at you cuz! You were great! You can still be great, and if you kick this addiction anything can be possible, man" Jimmy said, fighting back his tears.

"I need you! Mom needs you! Lil Leon needs you!"

Legend stood up from the filthy mattress and said, "Cuz follow me to the door."

The look inside of Legend's glassy eyes made it clear he was high.

"Jimmy, I love you like a little brother, and you know this, but I'm gone, and my life will never be the same. The drugs got a hold on me cuz, and I can't be saved.   The only thing in this life that makes me feel good is the drugs I put into my   system. Listen, I'll see you at the next game but for now, please just stay away from me."

Legend stood and watched as Jimmy walked out and got back into his car, before driving away. A lone tear fell from Legend's right eye, as he wiped it away and walked back into the room. Sadness covered his face as he got back on the soiled mattress and reached for the fork so he could eat the few collard greens that were left.

"Are you okay, Daddy?"

"I'm good. Where is the lighter?" Legend asked.

"It's right here, babe," Nicki said, passing Legend a small pink BIC lighter from out of her pants.

Legend reached into his pocket and took out a small crack vial and his glass pipe.

"You ready, baby girl? I need a hit then I'll eat the rest of this food."

"Of course, I'm ready!" Nicki said, excitingly as she sat up awaiting her turn.

Legend placed the plate of food on the mattress as he and Nicki started to smoke and get high together.

When the couple had smoked up all of the crack cocaine, Legend ate the rest of the food, and then they had sex on the filthy mattress until reaching their climax.

"Baby, can I ask you something serious?" Nicki said.

"What is it?" Legend said, still high and weak from his powerful orgasm.

"How did you end up here? I used to watch you play ball, and you was great!"

Legend was quiet as he pondered Nicki's question. He felt somewhat offended as his thoughts begin to circulate in his mind.

"First, you tell me how you ended up here. You were one of the most beautiful   girls in the hood. Everybody wanted pretty Nicki, including me. So tell me first,   then I'll tell you."

Nicki looked at Legend and said, "After losing my last three kids to miscarriages I needed an escape. I didn't want to think about what was wrong with me and why I couldn't carry no kids, so when a friend asked me to try some crack, I did. He promised it would take all my pain away and so my stupid ass tried it. I've been hooked ever since. I guess you can say I'm lost and turned out now. Ok, now your turn."

Nineteen-year-old Leon Shaw was the talk of the campus. After a rigorous four hours long practice, Leon raced back to his dorm to shower and get dressed. He had a hot date with a young woman he met named Kristen. She was an attractive Caucasian young female who would soon be graduating with a degree in accounting. Her long, flowing blonde hair, piercing blue eyes, and tall but slender frame made Kristen look like a model from the pages of ELLE magazine.

Kristen had taken notice of Leon at one of the games where he posted a triple-double. Since Kristen was a pre-teen, she had a thing for black men, and Leon now had her attention. Before approaching Leon, she came to the games as a spectator and simply watched. She saw that he was a lady's man, and with his skills, he could easily earn himself a one-way ticket to the NBA. Kristen was determined to make Leon hers, and she was the type of woman who always got her man!

After getting cleaned and dressed, Leon drove over to Kristen's apartment. Kristen lived in a private condominium complex near downtown Durham. She was the only child of a wealthy couple from Los Angeles, California. Both of her parents were well-known surgeons, and Kristen had lived a spoiled and prestigious life. With so much money at her disposal, she never worried about bills or where her next dollar would come from.

When Leon pulled his car up to the huge gate, he pressed the button on the security intercom and was immediately buzzed in. As the large gates swung open, Leon slowly drove his car on the newly paved entryway, which was surrounded by well-manicured grounds.

After parking, Leon walked over to Kristen's condo, where she had been patiently awaiting his arrival.

Once inside the luxurious home, Leon instantly noticed Kristen standing with a big, flirty smile painted on her face. She was dressed in a black Victoria's Secret lingerie set, and she had on a pair of Christian Louboutin's heels while holding a glass of red wine in her right hand.

"Hey, Daddy, why don't you get comfortable. We got all night."

Leon smiled and walked over and sat down on the couch. Kristen followed and sat beside him.

"I got something special for you tonight."

"Oh, really?" Leon asked as the look of curiosity grew on his face.

"Yes Daddy," Kristen said, as she placed her wine on the table before starting to undress Legend.

Leon watched as Kristen slid down his sweats and took off his tee-shirt. Without hesitation, his rock-hard dick was deep down Kristen's throat. Legend fell deep into the couch, drifting away in pure ecstasy.

Kristen was a professional, using the perfect amount of suction, adding the right amount of moans and making sure her throat was slippery as her saliva covered every inch of Leon's dick.

"Now it's time for that special gift I have for you."

Leon followed Kristen into her bedroom, and once inside, he was in surprised by what he saw. Laying across Kristen's king sized bed, was a beautiful redhead. Amy's nude frame was enticing as she smiled at Leon and blew soft kisses his way.

Kristen pushed Leon on the bed and said, "Tonight we're going to have some real fun. I hope you're up to it because we play hard."

"Don't worry, I can handle it," Leon said.

Amy reached under the pillow and took out a thin glass pipe and a piece of crack cocaine.

"What's that?"
"It's heaven, Daddy. Do you want to go there with us, or are you scared?" Kristen asked.

Legend thought about what they were offering him. He didn't know what it was, but at the same time, he didn't think it would be such a big deal.

Leon looked at the two beautiful women beside him and said, "I'm from Philly, don't nothing scare me!"

For the next few hours, the three of them fucked and got high off of crack cocaine. This would be the first encounter Leon had with the powerful narcotic, crack cocaine, and the beginning of his tragic fall from the top.

CHAPTER 7

It only took a few short weeks for Leon "Legend" Shaw to become addicted to crack cocaine. As his drug use became prominent, Leon began missing classes and his beloved basketball practices. Everyone on campus noticed that something was wrong with their star freshman basketball player. Leon's coaches and teachers also noticed there was a problem and tried to intervene, but to no avail. Legend was hooked, and there was nothing no one could do to turn back the hands of time.

After failing two mandatory drug tests Legend was expelled from school, and the national news picked up the story. Upon the airing of his fall from grace, it was inevitable that his quest for fame, success and basketball glory came to a predictable end. He also lost Kristen and Amy.

A few weeks later, Legend was back home in West Philly. To his community, family and the entire city of Brotherly Love who had had high hopes for the basketball prodigy, he was now viewed as a disgrace.

Within a year, Legend had become a new father, a drug addict, and a basketball has been. No one could predict this downfall. Legend was the golden child who carried a get-out-of-the-ghetto-and-straight-to-the-NBA pass. All he had to do was stay focused and uninjured, and he'd make it in; he was that good.

Since being back home, Legend moved back in with his Aunt Rose and his cousin, Jimmy. He battled bouts of severe depression and anxiety and tried his best to stay away from everyone who loved and cared about him. Legend's only escape was the crack cocaine that was destroying his body but numbing his mind and emotions. Crack was all he had left, and it became Legend's God and his demon.

CHAPTER 8

Once the crack was smoked up, Legend and Nicki left the abandoned building in search of a way to get high. They were feening for a hit as they walked around with dry crusted lips and wide opened red eyes; looking like two zombies from The Walking Dead.

Legend noticed two young drug dealers he knew standing outside of a crack house on 44th Street. He approached the young men and said, "Wassup Lil Kenny and Ray-Ray, I need a favor."

"Come on Legend, you still owe us from the last time you got drugs from us," Ray-Ray said.
"But, I got another game in a few days. Y'all know I'm good. As soon as I get paid, I will drop y'all money off. All of it," Legend promised.

Lil Kenny ran over to his hidden drug stash and grabbed a small crack vial.

"That's a dime, and that's all you're getting until you pay that forty bucks back   that you still owe us."

Ray-Ray and Lil Kenny looked over at Nicki with lustful eyes. She was the only crack head from around the way that they didn't have sex with.

"But we can erase your whole tab and give you another dime bag if you let us   fuck shorty. She fine as shit to be a crack head," Ray-Ray said with a devilish smirk.

"Hell no! Y'all better find some other chick," Nicki shouted.

Legend grabbed Nicki by the arm and pulled her to the side. After whispering something in her ear, they walked back over to Ray-Ray and Lil Kenny.

"Okay, y'all got ten minutes, and that's it," Legend said.

Nicki felt humiliated and dirty as the man lusted after her.

"Come on, shorty, follow us in the house," Ray-Ray told her.

Legend stood outside and watched as Nicki followed the men into the crack house. He cared deeply for Nicki, but not as much as he did for the drugs that ruled his life.

When they got into a room, inside of the crack house, Ray-Ray, Lil Kenny and Nicki got naked. Even though Nicki was a drug addict, she was good looking, and her slender body had some slight curves to it.

Ray-Ray tossed Nicki down on a mattress and spread her legs open as he slid his hard dick deep inside her pussy. At the same time, Lil Kenny knelt down overtop of Nicki's face and pushed his dick inside of her mouth. For the next twenty minutes, they used and abused every part of Nicki's body; fucking her raw in every hole she had. Nicki felt totally violated, and it was eating at her troubled soul, but she thought about the high she would get with Legend once the men finished having their way with her.

When it was finally over, Nicki rushed back outside. Lil Kenny and Ray-Ray laughed as they walked behind her. Nicki ran passed Legend and ignored him as he called her name out.

"Man, what did y'all do?" Legend asked in anger. "What the fuck happened?" "We ain't do nothing, but fuck her," Ray-Ray answered.

"Here's your drugs man," Lil Kenny said, passing the crack vial to Legend.

Legend was fuming, but he knew it was best to keep his cool. Both men were packing guns, and they also worked for Chuck and Mack- the two biggest drug dealers in the neighborhood.

Legend walked away and started to look for Nicki. He searched all the crack houses around the hood, but couldn't find her. Legend went back to the abandoned building he was staying in and got high, by himself.

Legend's mind thought back to Ray-Ray and Lil Kenny. They had a previous falling out over the eighty-dollar debt he owed them. The guys beat and stumped Legend out pretty bad, as a way to teach him to pay what he owed. When his cousin Jimmy found out, he approached Ray-Ray and Lil Kenny. The situation escalated quickly, and Ray-Ray pulled out a gun on Jimmy and yelled, "Fuck that crack head!

Tell him to stop being late with our money. If he wants to get high, he has to pay!"

Jimmy walked off and went to talk to Mack and Chuck. He asked, "If Legend is all beat up, how can he play ball and win y'all them bets?"

After their conversation, Mack promised Jimmy his workers wouldn't bother Legend again, as long as he played basketball for their team. But that incident left a bad taste in Legend's mouth. He didn't like Ray-Ray and Lil Kenny, and would not forget what they had done to him.

CHAPTER 9
LATER THAT NIGHT

Legend sat on the front step of the building shivering. His eyes were bloodshot red because he hardly got any sleep. Many times he wished and prayed he could go back home and lay across his warm, cozy bed. But, after Aunt Rose kicked him out of the house, hard floors and dirty mattresses had become his new resting norms.

As Legend sat hoping and wishing for better sleeping arrangements, a young man pushing a shopping cart with miscellaneous items inside approached him.

"Wassup Skeet, you coming inside to sleep?" Legend asked.
"Naw man, me and a few other dudes are going by the old factory on June Street to steal some copper and aluminum."

Skeet looked at Legend; he knew he was feening for some drugs.

"You got some money, Legend?"
"Naw. I didn't play no games today, so I'm broke right now."
"Then you need to come with me. That copper and aluminum pay good money," Skeet said with a smile.

Legend thought about it and said, "Fuck it, let's go," before following Skeet down the street.

Just a few blocks away from the old factory a police car slowly pulled up on Legend and Skeet. Two male officers were inside the car, one African American and the other was Caucasian.

"Yo Legend! Yo Legend," the cop yelled out. Legend stopped and looked over. He saw a familiar face and said, "That's you, Terrell?"

The police car stopped, and a big, tall, muscular black man stepped out.

"Yeah man, it's me, Terrell," the cop said. Legend and Terrell shook hands and hugged each other.
"It's been years since I last saw you," Legend said.
"Yeah, I'm a cop now, and this is my district. You still balling? Because I was just telling my partner all about you. How you was like Jordan on the court when we played back in high school," Terrell said.
"Yeah, yeah, I'm still balling. I play in the summer pro league at Mill Creek playground."
"Cool, I gotta come check you out one day."

As the two talked about old times, Terrell's partner called him.

"Yo, Terrell we gotta head over to the old factory. There's a report that some guys are over there stealing the copper and aluminum."
"Damn. I gotta go Legend, but it was good to see you, and I will try to make one of your games", Terrell said, rushing over to the squad car.

Legend looked at Skeet, and they smiled. Then without saying a word, Skeet turned the cart around. They were happy they hadn't made it to the factory, because going to jail for stealing aluminum and copper wasn't something they wanted to do.

Inside a tinted black BMW, Chuck and Mack were parked by the Millcreek playground. A few moments later, a silver Mercedes pulled up behind them, and a young man stepped out. The short, dark-skinned, man was dressed in expensive clothes and had multiple gold chains hanging from his neck. He also wore a Rolex watch and a pair of Gucci sandals. Duke was another major player in the West Philly drug game, and he was also a known gambler. He would bet on almost anything, cards, dice, horses, any sporting games, and everything and anything that could add to his fortune.

Chuck and Mack stepped out the car and approached Duke. After shaking each other's hands, they got down to business.

"The game is tonight at 7 PM. How much you trying to bet this time?" Chuck asked.
"Y'all got me for twenty-five grand on the last game so let's double it back and make it an even fifty racks," Duke said.
"Bet!" Mack said.

They shook on the bet, and Duke got back into his car and drove away.

"That nigga is a cold sucka! He must like losing all of his money to us," Chuck said, as he and Mack got into the car.

"Make sure you call Jimmy and tell him to have Legend ready for the game. Tell him we'll give Legend another bonus if he win by five points."

Chuck called Jimmy's cell phone and left a message on the voicemail.

"We good," Chuck said.

Duke pulled his car over at the corner of 49th & Hoops. Then he took out his cellphone and placed a call.

"Hello boss, wassup?" A voice answered.
"Make sure y'all take care of that ASAP! I got fifty grand riding on the game tonight."
"We on it, boss," the man said before the line went dead.

With a big grin plastered on his face, Duke pulled off down the street.

CHAPTER 11
43RD STREET
WEST PHILLY

Holding onto his basketball, Lil Leon sat on his steps, filled with excitement because today was his thirteenth birthday. He couldn't wait to see his father so they could spend quality time together. His father was his idol, despite his addiction. He heard the stories of how great his father's basketball skills were, and Lil Leon dreamed of one day playing in the NBA.

Even though the pair rarely spent time together, Legend called often and visited his son whenever he could.

"Do you want to take a ride with me?" his mother Shelly asked.
"No mom, I'm gonna wait here until my Dad comes by. He promised me we could play basketball together for my birthday."
"Okay baby, but remember what happened last time."
"I know mom, but I saw him the other day, and he said he would practice my jump shot with me."

Shelly could only shake her head in disappointment because she had seen Legend break his promise to their son too often.

"I'll be back in a little bit," Shelly said, as she got into her car and drove off.

Lil Leon couldn't wait for his father to show up! Anticipation ran throughout the young boy's skinny body.

As he waited for his father, he played a game of Roblox on his phone to pass the time.

CHAPTER 12

For the last few days, Nicki had been running the streets and purposely avoiding Legend after the encounter with Ray-Ray and Lil Kenny. The feeling of betrayal and humiliation was stronger than her desire to get high. Legend had traded her dignity for crack, and it hurt her deeply.

Legend and Nicki had been in an on and off again relationship for the past year, and unbeknownst to Legend, Nicki had lost two of their children due to miscarriages. It was a throbbing pain she carried, and she kept that secret to herself.

After turning a few tricks to satisfy her crack habit, Nicki found an empty building and rushed inside to get high. She had never had anyone offer her up for sex. She had no problems with being paid for sex, but she had to decide where and with who. Right now, she had to smoke to ease the memories of her inability to carry children to term, and her anger and disappointment towards Legend.

~~~

Aunt Rose was a short, light-skinned heavyset woman with a face full of freckles. At sixty-five, she had lived through and seen a lot of heartache and trauma in her life. The streets of North Philly gave her tough-skin, and though she could be hardcore, she did have a soft spot.

Her only child, her son James -who she nicknamed Jimmy- was her heart. His father had no involvement in their lives. He had lived up to the definition to a true deadbeat dad. Aunt Rose was big on friends, and what family she had- she did her best to keep them close. So after the tragic car accident and death of her sister, she became the official guardian for Legend. She raised him as best she could, as her own.

It was Aunt Rose who first placed a basketball in Legend's hands. She attended all of his practices, home games, and tournaments. Her home was filled with hundreds of trophies and MVP awards that Legend had won over the years.

Once drugs entered Legend's life, Aunt Rose saw the devastation it caused. She was distraught upon learning Legend had been expelled from Duke University. All he had worked for was crumbling before her eyes, and she felt like she had failed her sister. There wasn't a day that went by where Aunt Rose didn't pray for an uplifting change in Legend's life.

~~~

After Jimmy clocked out of his post office, he rushed to his car and drove home. He was excited about the game happening tonight. His 42nd Street team was going head to head with the undefeated reigning champs, the 39th Street Hawks. Their star player Rain was a top 10 NBA lottery pick in the last draft.

The whole city was excited about this game! It was being discussed in all the barbershops and hair salons in the city.

After Jimmy got cleaned up and dressed, he was out the door. Now he had to go find Legend because, without him, they didn't stand a chance against the top team in the league.

The black Range Rover, with dark limo tint, drove slowly down the street. The two men inside had been canvassing the West Philly neighborhood, looking for someone in particular. Upon spotting Legend leaving out of an abandoned house near Belmont Avenue, they stooped.

"That's him right there," one of the men said. The driver quickly made a U-turn and pulled up as Legend walked down the street.

"Yo Legend, you got minute?" the guy asked.

Legend approached the Range Rover and said, "Wassup fella's?"

"We need a tester for this new batch of crack we just cooked up. You down?"

"Damn right, where is it?" Legend asked enthusiastically.

"Right here," the guy said, dangling a small bag in his hand.

"Get in you can try it out at our stash house. Its' a few blocks away," the man told Legend.

"Okay, but I got a very important game today. I need to be there."

"No problem Legend, we will drop you off after you try out our product out."

Legend got into the backseat of the Range Rover and shut the door behind him. He didn't know the two men, and he didn't care that they were strangers. All he was concerned about was getting a free high.

"Oh, yeah, and it's my son's birthday. So we gotta make this real quick."
"Okay, we hear you, Legend. Don't worry, you'll be right back," the driver said, with a devilish smirk on his face.

Twenty minutes later, the black Range Rover pulled up in front of a house on 58th & Cedar. Legend got out and followed the men inside into the basement.

After giving Legend the crack, they watched as he smoked it and his eyes rolled to the back of his head.

"Damn, that's good!" he said.
"Cool. We got a lot more where that came from," one of the guys laughed.

CHAPTER 14
47TH STREET
TWO HOURS LATER

"Legend! Yo Legend, are you in there?" Jimmy yelled out.

After yelling into the abandoned house, Jimmy decided to go inside.

"Yo Legend!"

A young man around the age of twenty-two approached Jimmy. He was gaunt and looked like a human skeleton. Drugs had taken over his body and mind.

"You got some crack or heroin boss?" the man asked as he stood scratching his arms and licking his dry lips.

"No. I'm here to find Legend. Did you see him?"

A confused looked grew upon the young man's face.

"Why is everybody looking for Legend today? Did he get in some trouble?"
"No, I'm his cousin, Jimmy. Did you see him?"
"Yeah, earlier today. A few hours ago," the young addict said.
"Where at? And who else was looking for him?"
"I was with Legend earlier today. Sometimes we get high together. He always   shares his drugs."
"Okay! I get it, but where he at?"
"Around 45th Street, near Belmont Avenue. But he left out the house then I saw..."
"You saw what?" Jimmy said, getting annoyed.

"I saw this black Range Rover pull up and Legend got inside."

"A Range Rover?"

"Yes, it was one of them new ones that just came out. I know my cars," the man said.

Jimmy felt something wasn't right. Legend rarely ever missed a game and would never go too far on game day.

"Is everything okay with Legend?" the man asked with a serious expression   plastered on his face.

"I hope so!"

Jimmy knew the only thing that would get Legend into a strange person's car was, crack. He was very concerned, and something was not adding up.

After Jimmy left the abandoned house, he drove all over the neighborhood searching for Legend, but he was nowhere in sight.

Jimmy drove over to the playground for his highly anticipated game. When he showed up without Legend, a look of worry stained the faces of fans and his teammates.

"Where's Legend?"

"Where's Legend? We need him."

People kept asking Jimmy about Legend's whereabouts. Jimmy had no answer for anyone.

"Yo, Jimmy, will Legend be here?" Coach Jones asked.

"I'm not sure, Coach. I couldn't find him anywhere," Jimmy replied.

"Really, that's crazy."

"I think someone happened to him. Something ain't right."

Suddenly Chuck and Mack approached Jimmy.

"Yo Jim, where the hell is your cousin?" Mack asked.
"I don't know man! I couldn't find him. But somebody said he got into a new black Range Rover and that was the last time they saw him", Jimmy replied.
"Fuck! We got 50 geez on this game!" Chuck snapped.

Everyone stood around talking; then Jimmy noticed as a silver Mercedes and a black Range Rover pulled up and parked outside of the playground. One man from the Mercedes and two men from the black Range Rover exited their vehicles and stood by the playground's gate.

"That's a black Range Rover right there!" Jimmy pointed.

Chuck and Mack turned around and saw Duke talking to two unknown men.

"That no good motherfucker! He did something to Legend. I can just feel it," Mack said.
"What are we gonna do?" Chuck said.

"Nothing right now. Hopefully, we can still win this game without Legend. But I'm one hundred percent sure that this nigga Duke is the reason Legend ain't show up," Mack said.

"Coach Jones, just put your best five out on the court. It's all good for now," Mack said.

CHAPTER 15
58TH STREET

Inside the dark, dingy basement, Legend was handcuffed to an old rusty radiator. A few feet away, a young, tall and lanky, fair-skinned man with short wavy hair watched him

"Man can you please let me go I have a game! Plus it's my son's birthday!"
"I can't," the guy said as he sat on the milk crate sipping on a Sprite.
"I was paid to watch you, and I can't let you go until I get a call. Sorry, man."
"Do you know who I am?" Legend asked.
"Yeah, I know who you are. You're Legend! I grew up watching you play! I was   one of your biggest fans when you were at Duke University. But what the fuck happened to you?"
"The drugs, Lil homie! The drugs got me, and I've never been able to break away!"

The man sat back, trying to figure out how Legend could throw his entire basketball career away for crack cocaine. When he was younger, he had posters of Legend hanging on his wall, and he always believed Legend was going to make it big. Now he was holding Legend captive inside of the basement of an old row house in West Philly.

"I'm sorry man! I'm just doing my job Legend."
"It's my son's birthday, man! I can't miss that. He's depending on me to be there!"
"I understand, but I got a job to do, Old G."

"Fuck, man! If I don't get out of here, I'm gonna let a lot of people down! My cousin Jimmy, my coach, my teammates, and more importantly, my son!"

"I can't do anything until I get that call. Sorry."

"Please, man! Please just let me go!" Legend cried out hysterically.

"I can't, man! If I let you go, then I die," the young man said as he stood up from the crate and walked up the stairs and out the basement.

CHAPTER 16
9:28 PM
LATER THAT NIGHT

Lil Leon stood up from the steps and sadly walked into the house. Shelly saw her precious son's face as the tears fell from his eyes.

> "Baby, don't worry, it will be okay. I'm so sorry", she said, doing her best to comfort him.
> "I'm cool mom. I'm going upstairs into my room."

Lil Leon kissed his mother on her cheek and then rushed upstairs to his room. Shelly sat on the couch, frustrated that her son has been lied to yet again, as she finished smoking her cigarette. She was fuming. Shelly knew how much Lil Leon loved his father, and she was tired of Legend disappointing him. As long as Legend was on drugs, Shelly knew her son would never be able to depend on his father.

Laying back on his bed, Lil Leon tossed his basketball up in the air. All he could do was cry and pray that one-day things would be much better. His father was his hero, but his hero constantly hurt him.

~~~

Jimmy and his team put up a good fight against the 39th Street Hawks, but their start player Rain was just too good to be stopped. When the game ended, Rain had 52 points, 14 rebounds, ten assists, and four blocks. The boisterous crowd watched as Rain put on a one-man show, filled with dunks and three-point shots. The crowd had now dubbed him *The New King of the Court*, taking the crown away from Legend.

After the game, Jimmy got into his car and drove around, looking for his cousin. He was legit worried and scared that something crazy had happened to Legend. He drove around for three hours and when he didn't find Legend, he went home and told Aunt Rose what had happened. His mom was scared and made him get on his knees as the two prayed for Legend's safety.

"It's in God's hands now Jimmy. So get some sleep because God will see us through this. There's nothing else you can do."

CHAPTER 17
1: 52 AM

Nerves filled Legend's body as the two men from the Range Rover approached him.

"You can release him now," they instructed the young man who had been guarding him.
"You won us a lot of money tonight," one of the men said.

Once the young man removed the cuffs, Legend stood up. If he had a gun on him, he wouldn't hesitate to kill each man standing in the room.

As they all led Legend upstairs from the basement, he followed without saying a word. When he reached the front door, Legend took off running without looking back, as a light rain fell from the dark sky.

The streets were practically empty with only a few people out, as Legend slowed down to catch his breath. Even though he had no money on him, Legend tried to wave down a Septa Bus, but the driver kept going. He was exhausted from all the running he had done, and his heart was beating heavy inside of his chest. Legend took a few deep breaths and then continued to run to safety in the rain.

Twenty minutes later, he had finally reached his destination. Standing on the porch of Shelly's house, he began to ring the doorbell and bang on the door.

"Shelly, it's me Legend! Come open the door!' he yelled out.

Shelly looked out of her upstairs bedroom window and stuck her head out.

"What do you want, Legend! You missed your son's birthday! He waited up all night for you! Get the hell out of here and just go back where you was at," she yelled.
"I was kidnapped, Shelly! Two guys kidnapped me right before the game! I swear!"
"Fuck you, Leon! Fuck you for always failing your son! I can't stand your black ass! Don't come back here until you leave them drugs alone," Shelly said as she slammed the window shut.

Lying across his bed in tears, Lil Leon had heard it all. His heart wanted to believe his father, but his father had lied so many times that his mind was telling him not to. In the quiet of his bedroom, he cried himself to sleep.

Legend put his head down and slowly walked away. He was heartbroken and devastated for missing his son's birthday.

After walking all night in the rain, Legend went to one of his favorite spots in the hood; an abandoned building near 43rd Street. As soon as he walked into the building, the first person he saw was Nicki. They hadn't seen each other since the day she ran off.

Nicki walked up to Legend and gave him a kiss and hug; clearly she had missed him.

"I got a twenty-five dollar rock baby," she said.
"Where is it at?"
Nicki reached into her jean pockets and took out a small white piece of crack cocaine.

"You got a pipe?" Legend asked.
"Yeah," she said, passing him a lighter and a small glass pipe.

Legend broke off a piece of the crack and placed it inside the pipe. After lighting it up, he placed the pipe into his mouth and quickly inhaled the cooking crack into his system. Nicki watched as Legend took a few long hits before he started coughing.

"Are you okay?"
"I'm fine babe; I needed that!"
"Where you been at? I been looking for you all day."
'I was kidnapped!"
"Kidnapped???"
"Yeah, but it's a long story, and I really don't feel like talking about it!"
"Okay. Well, let's get you out of these wet clothes and go lay down on the   mattress."

When they were finished smoking the crack, for the rest of the night they had sex in the small backroom of the abandoned building; as the sounds of hard thunder and rain drowned out the noises around them.

CHAPTER 18

Early the next morning, Legend and Nicki woke up and immediately started getting high thanks to their young friend who had stopped by with more crack cocaine. In a bedroom next to theirs, a group of heroin addicts were sticking used needles into their arms. The house was a gathering spot for drug addicts and homeless people. Though city officials had boarded up the house five times in the last three months, it still managed to be used for drug use.

After a quick crack high, Legend and Nicki left out the house and walked to the local Rec Center where they washed and cleaned themselves up. This was a part of their morning routine.

"I have to go see Jimmy, Babe. I will meet you at the spot a little later."
"Okay, but please be careful. I don't want you getting kidnapped again."
"I'm good. I promise, Babe."

After kissing and hugging, each other, Legend watched as Nicki turned and walked down the street. For a moment, he just stared at her. Legend thought about the last twenty-four hours, and he knew he had to change his life around or else, he might not get another chance.

"I have to stop this shit. I have to help Nicki and myself," Legend mumbled to himself, as he started walking up Lancaster Avenue.

As he walked up the crowded avenue, people were calling out his name and asking questions.

"Yo Legend, what happened to you last night?" a man shouted.

"Legend, you a sellout!" a boy said.

"Legend, how could you do your team like that?" another said.

"He's scared of Rain!" someone else yelled out.

"Rain is the new neighborhood star, anyway and he's going to the NBA!" a kid shouted.

Legend didn't respond. He walked on with his signature smile on his face, knowing on the inside, his reign as the hood basketball legend was over. The people had crowned Rain as their new star.

CHAPTER 19
MARRIOT HOTEL
CITYLINE AVENUE

As the silver Mercedes pulled up and parked, Duke took out his cellphone and placed a call.

"I'm out front homie," Duke said before ending the call.

Just a short time later, a tall, slim black man walked out of the hotel carrying a small Nike duffle bag. He got inside of Duke's car and shook his hand.

"Great game last night Rain. You destroyed them bums!" Duke said, pulling off as he headed to the Philadelphia Airport.
"Yeah, they couldn't stop me. But, you know what, if I'm keeping it one hundred, I wanted to play against Legend! I wanted to prove to the hood that I'm the better baller and dude is just a crackhead," Rain laughed.

Duke reached under his seat and pulled out a large stack of cash which was wrapped in a thick rubber band.

"He probably was scared to face you. That's why he ain't show up. You're going to the NBA, and he fucked his chance up years ago. Maybe he didn't want to get embarrassed by the new rising star. But, here. This is for last night's work. That's ten-grand homie."

"Thanks Duke. That's love, and look anytime you need just let me know and I'm there," Rain said putting the money in his duffle bag.
"When you coming back in town?" Duke asked, swerving through the congested   traffic on the expressway.
"In about a week, I gotta go do a basketball camp for Lebron out in Akron, Ohio, but I'll be back before you know it. Trust me, I'm gonna get that bum Legend on the court one day. "He can't run forever."

Duke just smiled and turned on the music for the rest of the ride. Rain was clueless as to the events that kept Legend away from the game. Duke knew he had too much money on the line to take any chances of losing the game. Even with Rain at the point, Legend was a force to be reckoned with-on crack or not. Besides the 50-grand bet he had with Chuck and Mack, he placed others bets on Rain beating legend, that let him walk away with a total purse of a hundred thousand dollars. Duke was a gambler but when it came to losing, he took no chances.

After dropping Rain off at the airport, Duke headed back to West Philly. He was a man who loved making money and had no qualms with being a ruthless snake. Duke did what he had to in order to stay at the top.

When Jimmy walked out of the back of the post office, Legend was waiting for him.

"Legend! Where you been man," Jimmy said, hugging his cousin and feeling happy and surprised to see him. "Man, I been looking all over for you. You missed the game!"

"I was kidnapped man! These dudes kidnapped me and took me to a house up 58th Street. They kept me there until the game was over."

"Do you know who they were?"

"No, but whoever it was they had a big bet on the game."

Jimmy just shook his head in disbelief.

"Well, we gonna find out who it was because Chuck and Mack are pissed off. They lost a lot of money on that game."

"Jimmy, we lost bad?"

"Real bad. That Rain is tough! He got game Legend!"

Jimmy and Legend walked over to Jimmy's car and got inside. Legend was thinking about Rain and knew he wanted a piece of the youngbul on the court. He had never lost his hunger to show someone what he could do on the courts.

"Everybody is calling him the new king of the court, but that's because I wasn't there."

"It's all good, Legend. You'll get your turn to shine. But, we definitely needed you at the game. He was crazy on the court but he's in the NBA so I guess we had to expect his performance."

"I'm really sorry I let everyone down. I know how important it was to beat the Hawks. Trust me, we will get them next time."

Jimmy pulled over and parked his car in an empty spot. He looked at his cousin and said, "Legend you really need to leave them drugs alone! You're gonna die on them streets one day if you continue to keep this up. I love you Legend and so many others do too. You're killing yourself using them drugs. Please let me take you to get some help! Please man! It's a new rehab on Lansdowne Avenue that I heard is real good. The only thing is once you go inside you're not allowed to leave for sixty days. But so what. It that's going to get you clean, you should do it.

You need to do this, or you'll end up like Peewee, Zark, E-way, and all the others that lost their lives to drugs, guns, or violence. Please, Legend let me take you. I just want you to live Legend."

Legend sat silently. He knew the recommendation his cousin was giving made sense, but he wasn't sure if he could quit. Legend felt lost, confused, and overwhelmed with pride and guilt. He knew Jimmy and Aunt Rose wanted the best for him, and a day didn't go by where he thought about having a better life. Legend wanted to have a relationship with his son, and he wanted his son to be able to depend on him.

"One day cuz, I promise. Just not today."
"Alright, but I'm gonna keep asking you."
"Shit, I know. Listen, drop me off at the playground."
"Why? Who's there?"
"Someone I need to see."

FIFTEEN MINUTES LATER

When Jimmy pulled up outside the playground, he saw a familiar face shooting jump shots all alone. He smiled and then gave his cousin Legend a hug, as he got out of the car. Legend watched as Jimmy pulled off down the street. Then he walked inside the playground towards Lil Leon.

"I'm sorry about your birthday, little man."
"Yeah. I know. You was kidnapped, right, Dad? I heard you tell it to my mom."
"You believe me, right?"

Lil Leon picked up his basketball and stared into his father's eyes.

"Dad, did you ever lie to me before?"
"Never! And I never will."
"Then, yes, I believe you. It's crazy though because you missed the biggest game of the summer and you missed my birthday. I knew something had to happen for you to miss them."

Legend gave his son a warm hug. Lil Leon was the light that shinned in his dark world.

"Listen, I don't ever want you to do or get involved with any drugs! You hear me?"

"Dad, I won't."

"I mean it, son!"

"Dad, I won't. I see what it did to you."

Legend nodded his head. His son was smart and focused on making something out of his life. Lil Leon made Legend proud to be a father.

"Did you see the game?"

"Just a little bit. When you didn't show up, I went back home."

"How was Rain?"

"He good Dad! He's real good. They couldn't stop him."

"Do you think I could've stopped him?"

Lil Leon smiled and started dribbling his ball. Then he shot a jump shot that was all net.

"Well, answer my question."

"Dad, with you in the game, you always make a difference! You're the goat! Rain is good, but I think you're better. Way better."

Legend cracked a smile upon hearing his son's kind and encouraging words.

"But I know one guy that's gonna be better than both of y'all!"

"Who is that?" Legend said, watching Lil Leon make another shot.

"Me! Baby Legend! Just watch!"

For the next few hours, Legend helped his son practice his jump shots and dribbling drills. Legend knew Lil Leon had skills at his young age and he wanted to help develop them.

When they were finished on the court, Legend walked his son home. Once they arrived, they sat on the porch and talked as Shelly watched from her upstairs window.

CHAPTER 21

When Legend got back around the way, he was on the hunt for his woman, Nicki. He searched all of their regular hangout spots, but he couldn't find her. Then he walked towards 44th Street, a known drug area, where crack and heroin addicts went to buy their drugs, and as soon as he turned the corner, he saw Nicki. Ray-Ray and Lil Kenny were pushing her out and made her fall to the ground. They were laughing at Nicki as she struggled to get up.

"Bitch next time don't be leaving your teeth marks on my dick!" Ray-Ray said.

"And go somewhere and clean ya stinking ass pussy," Lil Kenny added.

Legend quickly ran towards the house and helped Nicki up from off the ground. He was fuming with hatred and guilt.

"Y'all ain't have to push her like that!"
"Hey man, when this bitch come around here fucking and sucking for drugs, we can do whatever we want!" Ray-Ray said.
"Fuck y'all bastards!" Nicki shouted out.
"You did already bitch! Now get away from here and go clean my nut out your mouth!" Lil Kenny laughed.
"God is gonna get y'all for this," Legend said, as he and Nicki walked away.

"Fuck God! And fuck you too Legend! The only reason we don't fuck you up is because Chuck and Mack won't let us. If they didn't need you for them games we   would've been beat ya ass," Ray-Ray shouted as he and Lil Kenny walked back into the crack house and slammed the front door.

As Legend walked away with Nicki, he felt a deep sadness that he had never felt before. Looking in Nicki's watery eyes, he had to hold back his own tears. In that moment, Legend knew he had to help Nicki. However, helping Nicki meant he had to get help himself. He just didn't know if he was ready.

"Kidnapped! By who?" Mack asked Jimmy.
"I'm not sure who it was, but one thing I know is Legend was kidnapped because someone didn't want him at that game. He said it was a big bet on the Hawks   to win."

Mack and Chuck's anger was written all over their facial expressions.

"We was played by Duke! That nigga set us up and beat us for that fifty-grand!" Chuck snapped.
"Yeah, plus he had a few other bets. He set everyone up," Mack said.
"Well, I just wanted to run that by y'all. Legend didn't sell us out, and he definitely wanted to play against Rain."

After the conversation ended, Jimmy got back into his car and drove away.

"What are we gonna do now?" Chuck asked.

"We gotta get our damn money back. And we have to play Duke like he did us. But, Duke is a boss out here on these streets, so no matter how we get our money back, we have to be smart about it. We don't need no war out here. A lot of men will die if that happens", Mack replied.

Chuck nodded his head in agreement. He knew Mack spoke the truth and getting into a war with Duke and his crew would bring a lot of bloodshed, and unnecessary heat from the cops. The neighborhood was already on the police's

radar due to the amount of guns and drugs on the street. They would have to be meticulous in their plan to get back at Duke so they could get their money back.

LATER THAT NIGHT

Inside the abandoned house on 42nd Street, Legend and Jimmy were talking.

"Here's some food my mom cooked for you," Jimmy said, passing Legend a large plate of food.

Then Jimmy reached under his shirt and pulled out a 38 pistol.

"This is for you too. Just in case someone tries to kidnap you again."
"Bet! I really felt scared for my life when that shit happened. This yours?"
"Don't worry about that. Just know it can't be traced back to either of us. You need to be safe out here, cuz. Everyone was worried about you when you disappeared."

After they shook hands, Jimmy left out the abandoned house and got back into his car and drove away.

Legend tucked the gun in his waistband; then he walked into a back room where Nicki was laying down on cardboard boxes. Nicki's eyes were filled with sadness, and there wasn't much Legend could say or do. He loved Nicki because she loved him, and she was loyal. Now, Legend knew it was his turn to be loyal to his woman.

As Legend laid down beside Nicki, she rested her head on his lap.

"We gotta go somewhere early in the morning."
"Okay babe, where to?" Nicki asked.
"I'm going to surprise you, babe. After we get cleaned up, I have to take you somewhere."
"That's fine babe, as long as I am with you, I don't care where you take me."

Nicki leaned up and kissed Legend on the lips. Within in moment, Nicki had fallen asleep on his lap. She slept peacefully as Legend ran his fingers through her long, silky black hair. Nicki was beautiful. She was mixed, her mother was white, and her father was black. If she had stayed away from drugs, she could have been a top model or anything else in life, besides a drug addict.

As a lonely tear dropped from Legend's eye, he said a silent prayer. He knew he was making the right decision, as he lay down beside Nicki and fell asleep.

CHAPTER 23
EARLY THE NEXT MORNING

The bright sun beamed its radiant light into the window of the abandoned house. As Legend and Nicki slept peacefully, a few mice ran across the floor and into the small holes in the baseboard. Other drug addicts lined the floors of the five-bedroom house. For many, this was home; until the city returned to board the building back up.

Many of these people were homeless and had been living on the streets for years. Their families had either turned their backs on them or given up hope they would get their lives together. They were known as "Nobody," because nobody gave a fuck about them anymore. Most had burned all their bridges with their constant lying and stealing. Their lives consisted of trying to find ways to get high, running from cops, and when they got caught, many continued to go in and out of jail.

When Legend and Nicki had awakened, they ate the food Jimmy had brought the previous night. The, after cleaning themselves up at Rec Center, Nicki followed Legend up to Lancaster Avenue.

"Babe, where are we going?" Legend didn't respond to Nicki's question. He was feeling guilty for what he was about do.

"Babe, are you okay? Why you not saying nothing?"

Legend refused to speak a single word. He knew what he had to do and didn't want to say anything. He needed to stay focused.

Thirty minutes later, Legend and Nicki walked up to a large white building on Lansdowne Avenue.

"What's this place? Who's in there?" Nicki asked.
"Just follow me Nicki," Legend told her.

Nicki entered into the building with Legend. Inside of the lobby were two huge male staff members dressed in white scrubs.

"Stay right here," Legend instructed Nicki as he walked over to the front desk where a middle-aged woman was sitting.

After writing down some information on a few papers, Legend pointed over to Nicki.

"That's her sitting over there."

The lady nodded her head at the two staff members and watched as they quickly approached Nicki. As tears ran from his eyes, Legend watched as the men grabbed Nicki by her arms.

"Baby, what are they doing to me? Babe, tell them to get off of me!" She cried out.

Nicki tried her best to escape, but the two men were too strong for her to overpower them.

"Legend! Legend! Legend!!!"

Nicki kicked, screamed, and tried to break free. It was hard for Legend to see Nicki crying and calling at his name, but he knew this was the best thing for her.

"Babe! Babe! Please don't leave me in here! Please!"

Legend watched as the two men carried Nicki through the large sliding doors. Then he turned and walked out of the building, and he could still hear Nicki's frantic screams.

Standing outside the rehab center, Legend was frozen. He hadn't felt pain like this in years. Hearing Nicki screams out his name was like feeling a sharp knife go through the heart. His mind was racing with unpleasant thoughts.

As Legend walked down the street, he could feel the weight of the .38 pistol dangling under his shirt. Everything in his life had gone wrong, but today, he decided to do something right.

Legend went by Jimmy's job and waited out front. He needed someone to talk to, and Jimmy had always been a good listener.

"What's up cuz?" Jimmy said.
"I did it!"
"You did what?" he asked, confused.
"I dropped Nicki off at the rehab center you told me about."
"You did?"
"Yeah. All I had to do was sign a few papers, and they kept her," Legend said, in a sad tone.

"So, what's wrong, then?" Jimmy asked as they got into Jimmy's car.

"She didn't want to go! She was crying and screaming out my name. It was killing me."

Jimmy looked over at Legend and said, "You did the right thing, cousin. You should be proud of yourself. Now hopefully one day it will be your turn."

"Yeah, maybe so. But not until I handle a few things first."

CHAPTER 24

Before dropping Legend off at the playground to practice with Lil Leon, Legend had Jimmy take him to an old abandoned house so he could hide the gun.

Legend had his son practice his jump shots and defense. Lil Leon also helped Legend tighten up his skills, as he passed him the ball at the top of the key and watch Legend run down several three-pointers.

"Dad, you would've destroyed Rain if you had played against him."
"You really think so, huh?" Legend said as he made ten jump shots in a row.
"I'm one hundred percent positive! I watch all your videos on YouTube, and I see you play in person, Rain can't walk in your sneakers Dad", Lil Leon said passing Legend the ball.

"Do you ever watch Rain games on YouTube?"
"A few times, but mostly I watch Kobe, Jordan, Lebron and you, Dad."
"Do you think I can watch a few videos on YouTube?"
"Yeah, we can go by my house now. My mom don't get off of work until five. We got a few hours. Come on Dad", Lil Leon said proudly.

Legend and Lil Leon walked to Lil Leon's house and went upstairs to his bedroom. The first thing Legend noticed was the posters of him, back when he was at the height of his game.

"Told you. You're my idol Dad," Lil Leon smiled.

As they sat down at the computer desk, Legend watched as Lil Leon logged into his YouTube account.

"I want to see some of Rain's videos," Legend said.
"In high school, college, or playground games?"
"All of them," Legend replied.

Lil Leon typed in Rain's basketball information, and they watched the videos for about an hour. When they were finished, Legend stood up with a big grin on his face and said, "He's weak when he goes to his left, and his defense is suspect. He goes for every pump fake!"

"You saw that?"
"Yes, and a few other flaws in his game."

Lil Leon walked his father to the front door. After they hugged, his dad promised they would link up in a few days.

As Legend walked down the street, he noticed a familiar face.

"Hey Rev?" he yelled to the short, dark-skinned man who walked out of an apartment building.

Legend approached the man and they hugged each other.

"Pastor Reynolds, it's so good to see you."
"You as well Leon! How have you been?" Pastor Reynolds asked as he looked Legend up and down.

"I've been good but I'm a little hungry. Can you spare a few dollars?" Legend said as he started scratching his neck and licking his dry lips.

Pastor Reynolds placed his hands on Legends shoulder and looked him deep into his hazel eyes.

"I'm sorry son, but I can't allow myself to feed your habit. I love you way too much to be a part of the devil's crew. I can't do it, Leon."
"I understand Rev, thanks anyway," he said, turning to walk away.

"Hey, Leon?"

When Legend turned around and looked back at the pastor

"When you're ready, I will always have a place for you, and my doors are always open."

Legend didn't respond. He nodded his head and walked away.

Legend was feening to have some crack in his system. The urge was killing him, and he could feel himself getting desperate. He tried to make some money by doing a few odd jobs; Legend came up empty-handed.

Walking down the street, Legend saw Ray-Ray and Lil Kenny beating up an older drug addict. He wished he still had his gun on him because he would have taught them a lesson they'd never forget. They were nothing more than bullies, who took advantage of the weak. And, for what they did to Nicki, along with beating him down, Legend wanted them to pay.

Legend watched from across the street as Ray-Ray and Lil Kenny pulled down the old man's pants and kicked him in the ass. The old man ran away, trying to get his pants up.

Ray-Ray saw Legend and said, "Where's your girl at? Tell her we miss that ass," as he and Lil Kenny laughed and went back inside of the drug house.

Inside of an abandoned house near 41st Street, Legend and his friend, Trey talked after they had finished smoking an eight ball of crack. The two had been good friends for years. Trey, who was forty-two years old, was a man who just couldn't stay out of jail. It was like his second home.

"You ain't tired of going back and forth to jail, Trey?"
"Hell yeah, but to be honest, I got caught on purpose."
"On purpose?"
"Yes! On purpose Legend. I get free food, clothes, shoes, and a roof over my head.   I usually get arrested in the winter and then I'm back out in the summer," Trey said as they started laughing.
"You crazy man. But fuck it, if it works why not?"

Trey nodded his head and asked, "Where's Nicki? Y'all like Bonnie and Clyde.

"She still around, just taking a little vacay right now," Legend answered sadly.
"You okay?"
"I'm good," Legend said.
"You sure? You need my help with anything?"
"Nah, I'm good homie. What I have to do, I have to do alone."

Trey could sense that something was wrong with Legend by watching his demeanor. He didn't know what it was, but his friend did not want to say. Instead of pressuring Legend to speak up about the issues that were bothering him, Trey changed the subject.

"When is your next game?"

"I'm not sure yet, but Jimmy will let me know."

"I heard y'all lost to the Hawks and you didn't play. The streets are saying you were scared to play against Rain. Let me find out you afraid of that rookie. Hell, he used to watch you play a few years back.

"Nigga you know I ain't afraid of no man walking on earth! And I damn sure ain't ducking Rain. Don't worry he's gonna get it!"

"Now that's what I'm talking about, we have to show these young bucks that we still got it! You have to take your crown back."

Legend nodded his head in agreement before saying goodbye to his friend and headed out to handle some very personal business.

The night was calm, and a light breeze blew against Legends face. As he turned the corner near 42nd Street, he walked through a maze of dirty alleyways until he found his destination.

Legend climbed a small wooden fence and slowly crept up the back steps. The back door was locked, but with a slight push, the old door gave in, and he quietly entered the house. Condom wrappers, soda cans, and other trash cluttered the floor. In the front room, he could hear men talking and laughing. As he tip-toed towards the voices, he took out his .38 and gripped it tightly in his right hand.

Legend entered the living room with his gun drawn and saw the two men sitting at a table counting stacks of money — each threw their hands in the air after being caught off guard. For the first time, Legend saw fear in the eyes of Lil Kenny and Ray-Ray. He felt powerful, and that was a feeling he wasn't used to.

"Legend just take the money! Don't kill us, man!" Ray-Ray said.

"Nigga are you crazy? This is Chuck and Mack's money! They will kill you and   your whole family if they find out you robbed us!" Lil Kenny shouted.

"What do you want man? The drugs are over there behind the couch. Just don't kill us, man!" Ray-Ray said.

Legend never spoke. He looked at the two cowards and realized how weak they were. Selling drugs and brandishing guns gave them limited power, but without either, they were two punks who took advantage of the less fortunate.

"Is this about your girl? A fucking trick?" Ray-Ray asked.

Legend walked close and pointed the gun at Ray-Ray's head.

"The last time I saw you two, I told y'all God was going to get you. And today I'm God," Legend said as he squeezed the trigger and unloaded every bullet in the chamber into Ray-Ray's and Lil Kenny's heads and chest. Death came instantly, and Legend watched as their bodies slumped down to the floor.

Nervousness rushed throughout Legend's body as he ran behind the couch and grabbed a black backpack from off of the floor. When he looked inside, he saw a large plastic Ziploc bag filled with crack vials. He quickly raced over to the table and started to fill the bag with the stacks of money. It was the most money Legend had ever seen, and upon filling up the bag, he quickly exited the house through the back door. Legend raced through the alley feeling that he had gotten away with a double homicide and robbery.

However, Legend had left a potential witness. There was an older man who was hanging around the back of the crack house. He was an addict and always scavenged through the trash for a good find. When he heard the gunshots, he hid behind a large trashcan. When Legend rushed from the house, the man recognized him.

Twenty minutes later, Legend was in the backyard of his Aunt Rose's house. He urgently called out Jimmy's name. Jimmy got out of bed and looked out of his window. He was shocked to see Legend standing in the yard, with the large backpack.

Jimmy quickly put on a shirt, a pair of pants, and his sneakers before walking outside to see what was going on. When he approached Legend, he knew something was wrong.

"Jimmy, I did something real fucked up!"

As Legend shared the horrific details to his cousin Jimmy, he was shocked. He didn't know what to do or to say. But, he knew they needed to get out of sight, so they rushed into the basement to count up the cash. There was over twenty-thousand in cash and about fifteen-thousand in drugs.

"Legend, did anyone see you?"
"No, it was just us there, and I left out the back."
"I'll hold this for you, and I know someone who will take these drugs off your hands. We have to get rid of this gun too!"

The two got inside of Jimmy's car and drove down to the Girard Avenue Bridge, and tossed the gun into the Schuylkill River. Jimmy saw an iron trashcan in a dump area, and he placed the backpack inside and burned it.

Inside the car, Jimmy said, "You can't tell a soul about this! If Mack and Chuck find out what you did, you're dead!"

85

Jimmy DaSaint

Inside the rehab facility, Nicki was having a tough time adjusting to her new surroundings. She didn't know anyone, and she felt alone. However, the staff was friendly, but Nicki refused to trust anyone. A few times, she tried to escape, but she was caught by staff and taken back to her room.

Sitting inside her room with two other drug addicts, all Nicki could think about was Legend and getting high. She felt lost without him, and it showed on her face. At night she cried heavily and had nightmares. Sometimes she'd wake up in a cold sweat as her body went through withdrawal.

Everyone at the rehab wanted to help Nicki, but she didn't want help. Nicki wanted to go back to the life she lived daily, of using drugs, tricking, and laying up with Legend.

"We can't help you unless you're willing to help yourself," a female staffer said to Nicki. "Fuck you! Just let me leave," Nicki shouted as she walked out of her room and into the lobby.

Nicki felt as if Legend had betrayed her. Even though she understood he wanted to help her, she did not agree with the way he went about it.

~~~

Mack and Chuck watched in anger as policeman carried the corpses of Ray-Ray and Lil Kenny out of the abandoned building. Police were calling the crime a drug-related robbery.

A small crowd gathered around the house and watched as the black coroner's van closed the back door, and the drove away.

"We have to find out who did this!" Mack said.

"It could've been anybody. Stickup boys, crackheads, other dealers or anybody   who had a beef with Ray-Ray and Lil Kenny. Those knuckleheads had enemies   every damn where. We don't know where to start looking. But, in the meantime,   we need to get two new youngsters that want work. The money can't stop, even   if bodies drop."

Mack and Chuck contemplated their next move before getting into their car and pulling off. They had taken a big loss with Duke and now this. Someone had to pay up; very soon.

CHAPTER 27

For two days, Legend stayed hidden inside the abandoned house with his friend Trey; getting high. He had taken a few of the crack vials from inside of the backpack. The only way Legend escaped his reality, was smoking crack. However, he felt no guilt for killing Ray-Ray and Lil Kenny. His guilt was for failing at life, for not being a better dad to his son, and for how he left Nicki at the rehab center.

Jimmy told Legend to lay low until things had calmed down. Detectives flooded the neighborhood asking questions about the double homicide. But, like most murder cases in the ghetto, they went unsolved and would be added to the overwhelming backlog of cold cases.

The following day, Jimmy picked Legend up for another game. Many of the fans were shocked to see Legend show up after he hadn't been present to face Rain. Once again, he would have to face another good baller named Jeff Johnson.

Jeff was a giant, standing 6'8, and he weighed a solid 260 lbs. He was a power forward who played for the Brooklyn Nets and had been in the NBA for ten years. Legend and Jeff had met a few times before on the court, and Legend always managed to edge out the NBA star.

Today would be no different as Legend put on a hell of a basketball show. He guarded and crossed over Jeff with ease, leaving the NBA star stunned. But this time Legend no longer had the crowd's support. Whenever he scored or got the rebound, the crowd booed him and shouted, "You scared of Rain!" Legend managed to block out the noise and continued to torch Jeff and his team.

By the fourth quarter, Legend had thirty-two points, six assists, and nine rebounds, guaranteeing a win for his team. Standing behind the bench, Mack and Chuck, cheered on Legend each time he scored. They had no clue they were cheering for the man who had murdered their workers and stolen their product and money. Their focus was only on the 25K bet they had on Legend to win the game, and with five minutes left in the game, they were going to have a good payday.

CHAPTER 28

When the game ended, Legend got back into Jimmy's car, and they drove off.

> "Good game cuz! You destroyed them bums!"
> "Yeah, but everyone was yelling Rain's name. They think I'm scared of him and they don't love me anymore because they think I quit on them because of Rain!"
> "Man, don't worry about that cousin, they trippin. And, hopefully, one day you will get your chance to prove them wrong."
> "When do we play against the Hawks again?"
> "We don't. We only play them if we meet up in the championship. But, I'm not even sure Rain will play in that game."
> "Why not?"
> "Because he's doing basketball camps all summer long with his NBA team."

Legend was disappointed. He knew the only way he could get his crown back was by facing Rain on the court. He wanted that chance.

Jimmy dropped Legend off on the corner of 43rd and Westminster Avenue. After he drove away, Legend walked through an alleyway and entered into the abandoned building from the back door. When he stepped inside the first thing that caught his attention was his Trey; who was sitting on the floor sticking a needle into his veins.

Trey had been a junkie and a crack addict for over twenty years, and he had no intentions or desires to get clean.

Legend stood there momentarily and watched as the powerful drug took Trey into another dimension. Then Trey began to shake uncontrollably, which he often did, as the heroin swept throughout his body. Legend was tired and exhausted from the game and needed to get some rest.

After finding his favorite corner in the house, Legend took out the leftover crack he had and placed it into a glass pipe. Moments later, Legend drifted away to a world of his own; blocking out the surrounding noises, and all the pain and guilt that lived inside of his troubled soul.

CHAPTER 29
EARLY THE NEXT MORNING

Legend was awakened by the sounds of screams and loud noises. When he stepped out of the room, he saw EMT's and police officers all over the place. There was a small group of drug addicts standing around with somber looks on their faces.

"What happened?" Legend asked one of the older addicts.

"Trey died," he answered sadly.

"What? Trey is dead? How?" Legend asked, confused because he had just seen his friend.

"He must've took a bad batch of that shit he be putting in his veins! We found his body early this morning. It was cold, and his eyes were wide open," the man said as they stood back and watched as the EMT's carried Trey's lifeless body away.

"That's Trey under that sheet?" Legend shouted.

"Not Trey! Damn, Trey," Legend said, shaking his head in total disbelief.

Legend and Trey had been friends for a long time and the sight of his lifeless body being carried away really messed him up.

After Trey's body was placed inside of an ambulance, the small group of drug addicts stood around grieving. Trey had been a member of their lost and hopeless community; but now like so many others, he was gone. He would be taken to the City's morgue where an identification tag would be placed on his big toe until his family came and claimed his body; if any one of them was willing to do so.

For the next hour, Legend walked around the neighborhood trying to clear his head. His week had been filled with a storm of pain, heartache, and drama.

Legend walked over to the local recreation center that had an indoor basketball court. The Rec's supervisor was a big fan of Legend, and he let Legend use the gym whenever he wanted to. Legend had been playing inside of that gym since he was ten years old. It was his escape and solace.

As Legend continued to shoot jump shots and dunk the ball, an epiphany came to him. Legend grabbed the ball from off the floor and walked over to the middle of the court, and said, "That's it! I know what I have to do."

"Are you sure, Legend?" Jimmy said as a shocked look sat on his face.

"Yes, I'm sure, Jimmy! I'm dead serious! I can beat him just set it up," Legend said.

"Okay cuz, I will call Mack and Chuck and see if they can get in touch with Duke and Rain."

"How much money do we got?" Legend asked.

"I counted thirty-thousand, and I sold the drugs to a friend for seven-thousand."

"Okay, I will let you know how much to bet on me," Legend said.

"You're gonna bet on yourself against Rain? Legend, I promised to hold that money for you until you got cleaned up. Why do you want to take a chance at losing it?"

"Because if no one believes in me, I do! I know my capabilities and skills on the court, Jimmy. Please just trust me, cuz, I have to do this. I just have to."

Jimmy saw the seriousness in Legend's facial expression and his words. He felt his cousin might be biting off more than he could chew, but deep down inside, Jimmy believed in his cousin. Jimmy had witnessed Legend play some of his greatest games on the court, and he had beat the best and top rated. But Rain was younger and stronger, so there was some doubt inside of Jimmy.

After their conversation, Jimmy dropped Legend off at the playground to practice with Lil Leon. For the next few hours, the father and son played one-on-one and enjoyed some quality time with each other. These were the days that Lil Leon looked forward to because being with his father was all he ever wanted.

They played a game of H.O.R.S.E, and then Legend and Lil Leon walked over and sat down on the bench.

"I got something big coming up soon."
"What's that, Dad?"
"First, do you know how to sneak into the rec center?
"Yeah, I do it all the time. Why?"
"I might need a very big favor from you."
"What is it?"

Legend trusted his son with his master plan, and when he had finished telling him all about it, all Lil Leon could say was, "Wow!"

Legend walked his son home before returning to one of the abandoned buildings he slept in. The first thing he noticed were two police cars parked out front of the building. He watched as his friend, Officer Terrell, placed a few drug addicts into the back of his patrol car. Legend nervously approached.

"Terrell, what's going on?"
"Oh, we just rounding up a few suspects to question about that double homicide a few days ago."

Suddenly a white officer walked up and said, "What about him?" he said, pointing at Legend.

"No, he's good. Trust me. Legend is a baller not a killer," Officer Terrell replied with a smile.

Legend laughed and nodded his head as the white cop frowned and walked back to his patrol car.

"If you hear anything about these murders, give us a call. That's the detective's direct number," Officer Terrell said, passing Legend a card.

"Okay," Legend said, as he watched Terrell get into his cop car and pull off.

Legend was now feening for a hit because he needed to calm his nerves.

LATER THAT EVENING

Inside a crowded neighborhood bar on Lancaster Avenue, Jimmy walked straight to the back of the bar and sat down at a booth with Mack and Chuck.

"What is it, homie?" Mack said.
"Yeah, what's so important that you wanted to meet?" Chuck said as he sipped   on a glass of Henny.
"Legend wants to play Rain, one-on-one. He said y'all can bet whatever on him   and he promises to get all that money back that Duke got y'all for."

Mack and Chuck busted out in laughter.

"Are you fucking serious Jimmy? Rain will wash Legend in a one-on-one. That nigga is in the pros", Mack said.
"And Legend is somewhere in a crack house!" Chuck added with more laughter.

Jimmy was unbothered by their doubts.

"I'm dead serious, and I'm willing to bet my own money and put it on my cousin."

Mack and Chuck stopped laughing when they heard Jimmy bring up money.

"Oh, you for real, huh?" Mack asked.
"Yes, Legend has studied his game, and he found lots of weaknesses. And if nothing else, I believe him."
"Well he must've found flaws that the NBA didn't," Chuck said sarcastically.
"Y'all been eating off of Legend for years. How much money did my cousin make y'all off them bets? Thousands! And he never failed y'all once! And if Duke didn't kidnap him, who knows what would've happened. Legend's been good to y'all.   Y'all knew him for years, before the drugs and before he lost his chance at the NBA. So, if y'all still believe in him and his game, then help him this one time. And not by giving him crack and a couple of dollars. He wants his crown back and he believes he can get it. So do I!"

Mack and Chuck were speechless because they knew Jimmy was speaking the truth. They had made thousands off of Legend's skills, sweat, and tears, and this was a possible opportunity to make more.

"We will set it up, Jimmy. Just give us the numbers, and we will see if Duke and Rain agree to it. I ain't promising shit, but we will try," Chuck said.

As a hard rain fell over the city of Philadelphia, dark grey clouds filled the sky with flashes of lightning and thunder. Legend was in deep thought as he stood by a window watching as the waterfall hard from the sky. Legend hadn't heard back from Jimmy about the five-thousand wager he placed on himself against, Rain.

Standing by the window, Legend couldn't help but think about the things surrounding his life. Nicki, Trey's death, and the blood that was now on his hands from killing Ray-Ray and Lil Kenny were recent events that only added to his troubled list. A lonely tear escaped his eye as Legend thought of what he could do to fix his problems. He knew what he had to do, but he avoided it. Only Legend could fix his problems, and even with the support and love from Lil Leon, Aunt Rose, Jimmy, and Nicki, he had to be the one to step up and get his life handled.

After the rain slowed down, a drizzle remained as Legend walked out of the abandoned house. Thirty minutes later, he walked through the doors of the rehab facility where Nicki was being held. After signing in, Legend was escorted to the small visitation room. When Nicki walked into the room, she saw Legend seated at a table. She quickly approached him, and they exchanged a kiss and a warm hug.

"I missed you so much," Nicki said tearfully.
"Missed you too," Legend said, noticing the difference in Nicki's appearance.

"You look, good Babe," he said, smiling.
"Thanks, Babe. I finally gave in and started going to counseling and listening to staff. They are real good here and very helpful. I want to say, thanks. I'm so glad you did what you did. It was the best thing for me. I feel so much better."
"You're welcome, Babe. I got some money for you when you get out of here."

"You do? Where did you get it?"
"Long story short, just know my cousin Jimmy is holding five-thousand for you as   soon as you get out. But, you got to promise me-no more drugs."
"I promise you! I'm done. Baby, this place was a miracle! A blessing in disguise and I can't thank you enough for what you did for me. Plus, they're helping us get a job when I leave here. So that money will definitely come in handy, and I promise you that I will never fall back into my old ways. I'm done with that life, for good. Now I'm just waiting for you to join me."

Legend didn't respond to her request, but he was very excited to be with his Nicki again. They continued to talk and enjoy their visit. When it was over, they hugged and held each other tightly, before Legend was escorted out of the facility.

SUNDAY MORNING

Pastor Lewis Reynolds had known Legend since he was a small child. His Aunt Rose used to bring Legend and Jimmy to his Baptist church- on Sunday. When he saw

Legend walk into the sanctuary and take a seat in the back row, a smile of joy and delight came to his face.

As Pastor Reynolds stood at the pulpit giving the sermon, he nodded his head towards Legend. Like everyone in the community, he knew Legend's tragic story. The pastor tried several times to reach out and help Legend, but he could never break the devil's tight grip that he had on Legend.

Legend stayed for the entire time, and when everyone left out of the church when the service ended, Legend and Pastor Reynolds sat down on a pew bench.

"It's so good to see you again son. How have you been since the last time I saw you?"
"I been good Rev. I just needed to hear the word. It's been a while," Legend said.
"Remember, I told you I'm always here for you. My doors are always open Leon."
"Thanks and I need something from you Rev."
"Leon, you know I can't contribute to your habit."
"No, I get that. I'm in need of your prayer, Rev! That's all I want is your prayers and maybe you can read me a scripture out the Bible."

Pastor Reynolds could only smile as he opened up his Bible and found a scripture to read.

"Yes, this is a good one. Isaiah 34:4. Tell everyone who is discouraged, be strong, and don't be afraid! God is coming to your rescue."

The short, powerful words caused Legend to fall down to his knees and bust out in tears.

"Don't worry son, God loves you," the pastor assured him.

After getting off the plane, Rain walked out of the American Airlines terminal and got into Duke's silver Mercedes Benz.

"Why you got that big smile on your face?" Rain asked.

"I got a sweet deal on the table. A way for us to make some quick cash."

"I hope it ain't nothing illegal man! I'm in the NBA now; they be on our ass if we get involved with illegal shit."

"It ain't nothing illegal, Rain. Someone wants to play you one-on-one."

"Who?"

"Legend."

Rain bust out in laughter.

"Are you serious? He can't hold my jock straps! I will bust that crackhead ass one on one."

"I know you will, that's why I accepted the challenge and the bet."

"How much is the bet for?" Rain asked.

"I told them niggas putting the money up, that you would only play a one-on-one game for a hundred grand, nothing less," Duke said, pulling onto the expressway.

"Did they accept the deal?"

"Of course. They suckas. If you can pull this off, I will give you twenty grand for breaking a sweat.

"Bet! I got this, trust me!"

"But there's a few rules."

"What's that?"

"They want to play the game in the old rec center, and no one can watch the game, but me and the two guys betting the big money. We will be the only ones allowed inside the gym. Plus, they said you have to beat Legend by two points since he is older and on drugs."

"Man, I don't care where we play, I'm gonna bust his ass, and he might not scorea point!" Rain said confidently.

"I hear that! I couldn't believe they called my phone with this stupid ass challenge. They are just giving me their money," Duke laughed.

"When is the game?"

"In two days, I will pick you up at the crib."

"I'll be ready."

Word spread quickly onto the streets that Legend and Rain were playing a one-on-one game at a secret location with no spectators. Jimmy had placed his bet with Mack and Chuck. Now all he could do was cross his fingers. As much as he believed in Legend, he knew taking the crown back from Rain would be easier said than done.

CHAPTER 33
52ND & PARKSIDE PLAYGROUND

"Is it true you're playing Rain one-on-one?" Coach Jones asked Legend as they stood around a group of ball players "Yeah, it's official."

"Where at? I need to see this game," Coach Jones said.

"I can't tell anyone. That's a part of the bet. Only the people betting the money   can be there."

"Rain is gonna kill you, man! He a dawg on that court," said a bystander.

"Legend, you might be biting off more than you can chew," another man added.

"How much is the bet?" the coach asked.

"A hundred grand!"

"Whoa! Somebody is gonna be sick after they lose their money," Coach said.

"How will we know who won the game?" another man asked.

"The streets will know when the game is over," Legend replied.

When Legend walked away from the court, he could hear the laughter and the jokes. No one believed in him, and they all thought he was way over his head, challenging Rain to a one-on-one game.

LATER THAT NIGHT

"Yo Legend! Yo Legend!" Jimmy yelled into the abandoned house.

"I'm back here!" Legend said.

Jimmy walked into a back room and saw Legend sitting in the dark alone.

"What's wrong cuz?"

"I'm nervous, man. For the first time in my life, I'm afraid of losing. So many   people are going against me, Jimmy. Maybe I made a mistake by challenging Rain."

Jimmy sat beside Legend and said, "You ain't never been scared a day in your life, so don't get scared on me now! You're the Legend, and you have to go out there tomorrow and prove that to everyone who doubted you!"

"I'm gonna try cuz. Trust me; I'm gonna do my best."

"Let's go Legend," Jimmy said as he stood up.

"Where?"

"You staying at the house with me tonight. I don't need nothing else happening to   you before tomorrow."

"What about Aunt Rose?"

"She said you can stay the night," Jimmy said, as a smile graced his face.

"Are you serious?"

"I'm dead serious!"

The smile that grew on Legend's face was the biggest smile he had had in a long time. Aunt Rose was like a mother to Legend, and for her to trust him to come back in her home, after he had disappointed her so many times, was priceless. Legend thought about taking a nice, warm shower, having a good home cooked meal at a table, and sleeping in a bed, and he was thrilled.

"Jimmy, what did you say to her?"

"I told her that you wanted another chance and that you promised you would   never steal from her again. And I told her about your game tomorrow against   Rain, and she agreed to let you come back, for the night.

As they walked out of the building, Legend tried his best to hold back his tears. He felt overwhelmed with joy and a sense of relief.

When Jimmy and Legend arrived at the house, Aunt Rose was inside of the living room waiting on them. Aunt Rose had missed Legend's presence, his helpfulness with household chores, and she enjoyed watching ESPN with her nephew. Legend's absence left a void in her heart and home.

Legend walked through the door, and Aunt Rose gave him a long, loving hug. Her tears overflowed as she looked into his eyes. Jimmy stood back, grinning. He knew how much his mother cared for Legend.

"I missed you so much, Leon! God knows I missed you, and I've prayed every day   for God to keep you safe while you're on them streets."
"I know Aunty; I heard all of your prayers."

After they ate dinner and had a lengthy conversation at the living room table, Aunt Rose and Jimmy went to their bedrooms. Legend took a warm, overdue shower and laid down across his large king size bed. He had forgotten how good the soft cotton sheets felt on his skin. His room was just like he had left it; filled with posters of NBA stars and stacks of Nike sneaker boxes up against the wall.

Legend said a prayer of thanks, even if this small blessing was only for a night, and then he drifted off into a deep sleep as the soft mattress hugged his body.

It was a perfect hot summer day as the temperature soared into the low 90's and the sun shined brightly. Legend and Jimmy awoke to a home cooked breakfast of pancakes, eggs, turkey sausages, and a fresh glass of orange juice.

When Aunt Rose left the house to run errands and pay a few bills, Jimmy and Legend began to get prepared for the game that started at 3 PM, sharp.

After the two got dressed, they stopped by Lil Leon's house. Legend needed to share a very important message with his son.

"Don't worry, Dad; I won't forget," Lil Leon said as Legend Jimmy pulled off.

Then they drove to the Foot Locker, and Jimmy bought Legend a new pair of Jordan's and a pair of black Nike basketball shorts. With each passing hour, Legend became more nervous. The anticipation was killing Legend, and once two o'clock arrived, they headed over to the recreation center.

Jimmy pulled up in front of the rec center, and the first thing he noticed was the silver Mercedes and the black BMW parked outside. Everyone stepped out of their cars, once Legend and Jimmy got out of the car, and they all walked towards the entrance of the building.

As Legend walked towards the door, he heard a voice call out his name. When he turned around, he saw a short, older man walking towards him.

"Do you got a minute Legend?"
"Not right now."
"Please, it's very important," the old man said.
"Give me a minute fellas; I'll be right there."

Jimmy was curious about what the older man wanted. He walked with the unexpected visitor and his cousin back to his car so that they could speak in private. Jimmy kept a close watch.

"What's up Old G?"
"My name is Willie, and I been watching you play for years."
"Yo, my cousin has a very important game waiting inside."
"I know all about the game; it's all over the streets, but that's not why I'm here."
"Then what is it?" Legend asked politely.
"I saw what you did!"
"What are you talking about?" Legend said, as confused by the man's statement.
"I was there at the crackhouse the night Ray-Ray, and Lil Kenny got murdered. I saw you run off with a backpack. I was hiding behind a trashcan. I saw you run   away through the alley."

Legend and Jimmy's jaws dropped. They couldn't believe what they were hearing.

"Fuck! So what do you want? Money?" Jimmy snapped, looking around to make sure no one else could hear them talking.

Legend was in total disbelief because he was certain he had gone unseen, but he was wrong.

"How much do you want, Mr. Willie?" Jimmy asked again.

The older man smiled broadly.

"What's so funny, Old G.?" Legend asked, trying to figure out why the man was smiling.
"I don't want nothing from y'all. Not one damn cent!"
"Huh?" Jimmy said.

Legend and Jimmy were utterly confused.

"Legend, I saw you that day."
"What day?"
"The day Ray-Ray and Lil Kenny took down my pants and kicked me in my ass. I saw you across the street. I saw the look in your eyes, and I knew you wanted to help me, but I ran off down the street. You saw me hurting, and you wanted to help an old man out. You showed me some respect, and I appreciate that.

The night I got my .22 pistol I went back to kill them sons-of-a-bitches! That's why I was hiding in the back of the house, but you beat me to it. So, I'm not here for any money. I'm here to say thank you Legend, and I promise you, son, that your secret is safe with me."

Legend was speechless as he shook the old man's hand and said, "Thank you."

Jimmy DaSaint

CHAPTER 35

Jimmy waited outside the recreation center as he paced back and forth. The rules were so strict that even he wasn't allowed inside to watch the game. He was nervous and sweating as he anticipated the outcome. Jimmy was dying to see what was going on inside.

Forty-five minutes had passed when the front door of the recreation center opened. Legend walked out with a stoic face and Jimmy rushed up to him.

"What happened???"

Before Legend could answer him, Duke and Rain walked out with disappointed and salty looks stained on their faces. Neither said a word as they walked pass Jimmy and Legend. They rushed into the silver Mercedes and sped off down the street. Then Mack and Chuck walked out the building, grinning.

"Yo, what happened?" Jimmy shouted out.
"I lost! I lost the game!" Legend said, but he had a big smile on his face.
"What was the score?" Jimmy asked.
"The score was 10-9; he beat me by one point."

Jimmy didn't know if he could believe what he was hearing. Why was Legend smiling if he had lost? Did he really lose the game?

"Are you serious? Tell me you're joking, Legend!"
"I'm not. It was down to the last shot, and he beat me by one point."

Jimmy took a moment to think about what his cousin was saying as a major fat dawned on him.

"Yo, you won the bet, Legend! Rain had to win the game by two points to win the money," Jimmy said with excitement.

Mack walked up to Jimmy and passed him a Nike sports bag.

"It's all there, Jimmy. Thanks for everything. We are gonna get out of here and go enjoy our winnings."

Legend saw the large bag, and he was confused.

When Mack and Chuck drove off, Legend rushed to talk to his cousin.

"Jimmy, what the hell is going on?"
"Legend, you did it! You did it!"
"Yeah, I won five-thousand, because Rain didn't beat me by two points. So what's the big deal?"
"Naw, you won more than five-thousand Legend."
Legend was lost.
"Jimmy what did you bet???"
"I bet it all on you. The whole thirty! You got 60K cousin!!!"

Legend was dumbfounded, he couldn't believe his ears as he joined in the excitement with his Jimmy.

"Are you fucking serious, Jimmy?"
"I'm dead serious cuz. I put it all on you! Every single penny! Mack and Chuck put seventy and I put up

thirty. I told them Rain had to beat you by two points to win the money and, both Duke and Rain agreed."

Jimmy opened up the Nike sports bag, and Legend saw the large sum of money inside.

"I knew the game would be close, but he couldn't blow you out. But, it's too bad no one could see you go down to the wire with Rain. Everyone said he would destroy you and you wouldn't get a single basket. They were wrong!"

Legend smiled, and then Lil Leon walked up from around the rec center.

"You get those pictures I asked you to take?"
"Yup."
"He was inside?" Jimmy asked.
"Yeah, he snuck in to take some pictures of the game. He was hiding behind the bleachers."
"So that's why you went by his house?"
"Yeah, I needed proof just in case I won the game.
"But pictures can't show nobody how close the game was," Jimmy said, as they walked over to his car.

"My dad is old school. I didn't get pictures; I got video."
"You did, son????"
"Yup! Got it all on my phone. Now the whole world can see just how good you are and how Rain got smoked."
 "How will the world know it's all on your phone?"

Lil Leon and Jimmy laughed.

"Dad, you gotta get up with the times. I put it on my YouTube channel. It already had over a thousand views."

"A thousand, what?"

"Look, Dad," Lil Leon said, showing his father the video and the mounting comments on his phone.

"Now all the haters will see that my dad is still the Legend!"

Legend couldn't believe his luck. His emotions were going in every direction, and he was overwhelmed with emotion. Today was a day filled with blessing, and he could not be more thankful for his newfound luck.

"How do you feel cuz?" Jimmy asked him.

"I feel good, Jimmy, and even though I lost the basketball game, I feel like I just won the game of life," Legend said as tears of appreciation fell from his eyes.

CHAPTER 36

After dropping Lil Leon off at home, Jimmy looked at Legend and said, "Now let's go celebrate."

"Where to, Legend? We can go anywhere you want to go."

Legend smiled as he looked at his cousin. He was thankful that Jimmy had continued to support and love him, despite his addiction and many downfalls.

"I'm ready cuz! I'm ready to go!"

"Great, where we going?

"It's time to fix my life," Legend said to his beloved cousin. Jimmy knew exactly where they were going. He had waited so long for his cousin to make this decision, and Jimmy smiled, as joy filled his heart.

"I'll hold all your money for you until you get out, cuz."

"Okay, I trust you, Jimmy. And make sure you take ten grand for yourself."

"Yo, man you serious?

"Dead serious. It's because of your faith in me that we won any money. If you hadn't come through and kept checking on me, feeding me, and keeping me on the court, this would have never happened. And then for you to bet big on me. A man that people laughed at. I man that forgot his own worth, someone who everyone labeled as just another crackhead; hell, yeah, you get that money. And you better enjoy it too."

Jimmy's tears spoke for his gratitude as the Ford Taurus pulled up and parked outside the front of the drug rehabilitation center on Lansdowne Avenue. Legend gave his cousins a long, thankful hug as he got out of the car and walking towards the entry door.

"See you in 60 days, Legend," Jimmy shouted out to his cousin as he walked into the rehab center with a confident expression on his face.

DaSaint
ENTERTAINMENT
WE SHIP TO PRISONS

BLACK SCARFACE

BLACK SCARFACE II

BLACK SCARFACE III

BLACK SCARFACE IV

DOC

KING

KING 2

KILLADELPHIA

ON EVERYTHING I LOVE

MONEY DESIRES & REGRETS

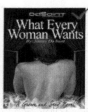

WHAT EVERY WOMAN WANTS

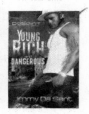

YOUNG RICH & DANGEROUS

THE UNDERWORLD

A ROSE AMONG THORNS

A ROSE AMONG THORNS 2

SEX SLAVE

DaSainT
ENTERTAINMENT
WE SHIP TO PRISONS

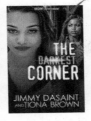

AIN'T NO SUNSHINE

WHO

THE DARKEST CORNER

HOTTEST SUMMER EVER

BLACK GOTTI

CONTRACT KILLER

THE 21 LESSONS OF LIFE

SOSA

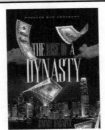

COMING SOON

LEGEND

THE RISE OF A DYNASTY

DASAINT ENTERTAINMENT SPECIALS

Orders being shipped to a **PRISON FACILITY ONLY**, qualify for the 3 for $30 Special! The books marked with a red checkmark can be purchased. This special **does not** include the BLACK SCARFACE Series, DOC, KING titles, The 21 Lessons of Life, SOSA or LEGEND. The flat rate shipping for these items are $8.00.

DASAINT ENTERTAINMENT REFUND POLICY

No Refunds Will Be Processed. All Sales Are Final!

If you submit the wrong address for any order or forget an inmate identification number, you must pay for shipping cost again, for those books to be redelivered.

If your item is returned to us by a prions facility, for any reason, you must pay to have those items shipped to another address. Return merchandize are held for ninety days. If they are not claimed by then, they will not be shipped out.

TITLE	PRICE	QTY
BLACK SCARFACE	$15.00	_____
BLACK SCARFACE II	$15.00	_____
BLACK SCARFACE III	$15.00	_____
BLACK SCARFACE IV	$15.00	_____
DOC	$15.00	_____
KING	$15.00	_____
KING 2	$15.00	_____
KILLADELPHIA	$15.00	_____
ON EVERYTHING I LOVE	$15.00	_____
MONEY DESIRES & REGRETS	$15.00	_____
WHAT EVERY WOMAN WANTS	$15.00	_____
YOUNG RICH & DANGEROUS	$15.00	_____
THE UNDERWORLD	$15.00	_____
A ROSE AMONG THORNS	$15.00	_____
A ROSE AMONG THORNS II	$15.00	_____
SEX SLAVE	$15.00	_____
AIN'T NO SUNSHINE	$15.00	_____
WHO	$15.00	_____
THE DARKEST CORNER	$15.00	_____
HOTTEST SUMMER EVER	$15.00	_____
BLACK GOTTI	$15.00	_____
CONTRACT KILLER	$15.00	_____
THE 21 LESSONS OF LIFE	$12.99	_____
LEGEND	$12.99	_____
SOSA	$15.00	_____

Fill out this form and send it to:

DASAINT ENTERTAINMENT
PO BOX 97
BALA CYNWYD, PA 19004

Make Money Orders payable to:
DASAINT ENTERTAINMENT (NO CHECKS ACCEPTED)

NAME: _____

ADDRESS: _____

_____

CITY: _____ STATE: _____ ZIP: _____

PHONE: _____ EMAIL: _____

PRISON ID NUMBER_____

$3.00 per item for Shipping and Handling
($5.00 per item for Expedited Shipping)

Please visit www.dasaintentertainment.com to place online orders.

WE SHIP TO PRISONS

DUPLICATE FORM

TITLE	PRICE	QTY
BLACK SCARFACE	$15.00	____
BLACK SCARFACE II	$15.00	____
BLACK SCARFACE III	$15.00	____
BLACK SCARFACE IV	$15.00	____
DOC	$15.00	____
KING	$15.00	____
KING 2	$15.00	____
KILLADELPHIA	$15.00	____
ON EVERYTHING I LOVE	$15.00	____
MONEY DESIRES & REGRETS	$15.00	____
WHAT EVERY WOMAN WANTS	$15.00	____
YOUNG RICH & DANGEROUS	$15.00	____
THE UNDERWORLD	$15.00	____
A ROSE AMONG THORNS	$15.00	____
A ROSE AMONG THORNS II	$15.00	____
SEX SLAVE	$15.00	____
AIN'T NO SUNSHINE	$15.00	____
WHO	$15.00	____
THE DARKEST CORNER	$15.00	____
HOTTEST SUMMER EVER	$15.00	____
BLACK GOTTI	$15.00	____
CONTRACT KILLER	$15.00	____
THE 21 LESSONS OF LIFE	$12.99	____
LEGEND	$12.99	____
SOSA	$15.00	____

Fill out this form and send it to:

DASAINT ENTERTAINMENT
PO BOX 97
BALA CYNWYD, PA 19004

Make Money Orders payable to:
DASAINT ENTERTAINMENT (NO CHECKS ACCEPTED)

NAME: _____

ADDRESS: _____

_____

CITY: _____ STATE: _____ ZIP: _____

PHONE:_____ EMAIL: _____

PRISON ID NUMBER_____

$3.00 per item for Shipping and Handling
($5.00 per item for Expedited Shipping)

Please visit www.dasaintentertainment.com to place online orders.

WE SHIP TO PRISONS

Made in the USA
Middletown, DE
15 February 2024

49873157R00073